ArtScroll Youth Series®

Rabbi Nosson Scherman / Rabbi Meir Zlotowitz

General Editors

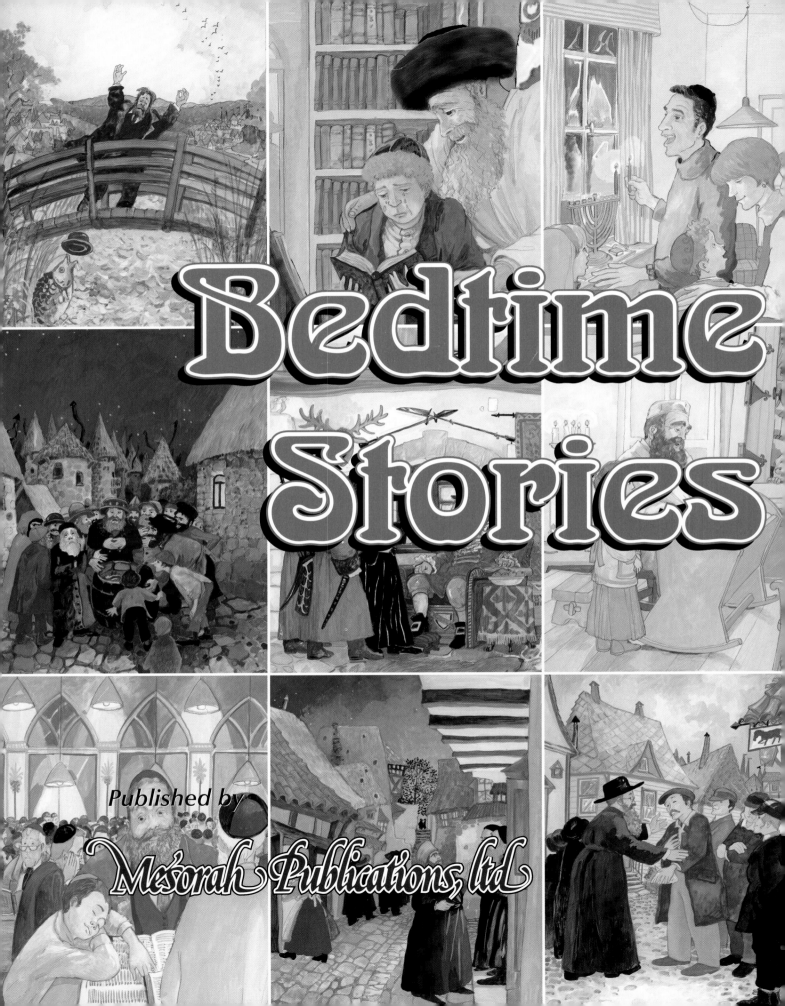

Bedtime Stories

Published by
Mesorah Publications, ltd

# of Jewish Holidays

by Shmuel Blitz

Illustrated by Liat Binayamini Ariel

This book is dedicated to my son
Avraham Uri Blitz

RTSCROLL YOUTH SERIES®

" BEDTIME STORIES OF JEWISH HOLIDAYS"

© *Copyright 1998 by* Mesorah Publications, Ltd.
First edition – First impression: November, 1998
   Second impression: November, 2001
   Third impression: May, 2005
   Fourth impression: April, 2010

Published by **MESORAH PUBLICATIONS, LTD.**
4401 Second Avenue / Brooklyn, N.Y 11232 / (718) 921-9000 / Fax: (718) 680-1875
www.artscroll.com

Distributed in Israel by SIFRIATI / A. GITLER
6 Hayarkon Street / Bnei Brak 51127

Distributed in Europe by J. LEHMANNS HEBREW BOOKSELLERS
Unit E, Viking Business Park, Rolling Mill Road / Jarrow, Tyne and Wear / England NE32 3DP

Distributed in Australia and New Zealand by GOLD'S BOOK & GIFT SHOP
3-13 William Street / Balaclava, Melbourne 3183, Victoria, Australia

Distributed in South Africa by KOLLEL BOOKSHOP
Shop 8A Norwood Hypermarket / Norwood 2196 / Johannesburg, South Africa

Custom bound by Sefercraft, Inc. / 4401 Second Avenue / Brooklyn, N.Y. 11232

ISBN 10: 1-57819-174-2 / ISBN 13: 978-1-57819-174-1

Table of Contents

SHABBOS
The Shabbos Fish

here once lived a man named Yosef. He loved Shabbos more than anything else. All week long he saved his money in order to buy the best food for Shabbos. "I only want the most delicious *kugels*, the tastiest desserts, and especially the most beautiful fish I can find in the market," thought Yosef. That is why people called him Yosef Mokir Shabbos, Yosef Who Honors the Shabbos.

A rich, miserly man lived in the same town as Yosef. This man was told that one day he would lose all his money to Yosef. The man became very worried. "I do not want to lose all my money to Yosef," he thought. "I know how to stop this from happening."

The man hurried into town and sold all his possessions. He took the money and bought a giant pearl — the most beautiful pearl anyone had ever seen. Then he sewed the pearl onto his hat. "I'll never let this hat out of my sight, not even for one minute," he said. "Now Yosef will not be able to get my money."

That day, as the man was crossing a bridge, a gust of wind blew his hat into the river below. "My hat, my hat," screamed the man. "Someone must save my hat." But a large fish swallowed the hat and swam away. "My entire fortune is lost," cried the miserly man.

That Friday a fisherman brought his whole catch of fish to the market to sell. The market was already almost empty. "How will I ever sell this last fish," he wondered. "It is so large, who would want to buy it?"

"Sell it to Yosef Mokir Shabbos," the people advised him. "He will surely buy your fish, because it is so splendid."

The fisherman brought the fish to Yosef. "This is the finest fish

I have ever seen. It is perfect for my Shabbos table," Yosef joyfully exclaimed. "I will happily buy it from you."

Yosef took a knife to prepare the fish for Shabbos. "What is this?" asked Yosef as he cut the fish open. Inside the fish, he found a hat with a pearl attached to it. Yosef was overjoyed. After Shabbos he brought the pearl to a jeweler and sold it for a large amount of money.

Our Sages teach us that Yosef received this reward because he honored the Shabbos so much.

But Never on Shabbos!

It was Friday night in Reb Mendel's home. The entire family sat around the table, eating delicious Shabbos food, discussing Torah topics, and singing *zemiros*. Suddenly, they heard a loud knock at the door.

Ten soldiers entered the house. "The baron sent us here," the leader barked. "You are a wine merchant, and he is having a large party tonight. We want to buy twenty cases of your most expensive wine, now."

"I would love to help him," replied Reb Mendel, "but I cannot do any business now. Tonight is the holy Sabbath."

"The baron is your best customer," the soldier thundered. "I warn you, you must sell him this wine, and he needs it tonight!"

"I am always happy to serve the baron, and he is, indeed, my best customer," answered Reb Mendel, "but never on Shabbos."

The soldiers left. Reb Mendel's son asked, "But couldn't you have given them the key to your warehouse and charged him on Sunday?"

"I have never done business on the holy Shabbos, and I will not start today," Reb Mendel explained to his son.

The soldiers returned two more times that evening, demanding the twenty cases of wine. But each time Reb Mendel refused.

Sunday morning, Reb Mendel was summoned to the baron's castle. "Friday night," the baron said, "I wanted you to sell me twenty cases of your finest wine. But you refused."

Reb Mendel stood tall and replied, "You are my best customer, honored baron, but I do not do business on the Sabbath. Never."

A smile appeared on the baron's face. "Now let me tell you the rest of the story," he explained. "Friday morning, the count from the next village visited me. 'Jews only care about money,' he claimed. I said this wasn't true. He insisted you would sell me twenty cases of wine, even though it was your Sabbath. I made him a large bet, twenty gold coins, that you would not violate your Sabbath at any cost. So you see, because of your devotion to the Sabbath, I have won a large amount of money."

"And more important," thought Reb Mendel, "Shabbos was truly honored."

ROSH HASHANAH
Higher than High

The entire week before Rosh Hashanah, everyone in the village of Nemirov would awaken before dawn, go to *shul*, and recite the *Selichos* prayers.

After *davening*, the Rebbe of Nemirov rushed out of *shul*. "The rebbe is hurrying because he rises straight up to heaven to pray for us," the people said.

But little Yankel wanted to see this for himself. He followed the rebbe home, hoping to see him rise up to heaven. Then he peeked into the window as the rebbe entered his house. He saw the rebbe put on an old tattered woolen coat. "What could the rebbe be doing?" thought Yankel. Then he saw the rebbe go to his closet and take out an axe. This confused Yankel even more.

Leaving his house, the rebbe headed towards the forest. Yankel quietly followed, making sure he couldn't be heard. The rebbe took his axe and chopped down a small tree. He then cut the tree into small pieces, tied them together and loaded them on his back.

Yankel followed the rebbe deeper and deeper into the forest until they came to an old hut. The rebbe called into the hut, "It is Zlasik the woodcutter. I have brought you wood for the winter."

Yankel stared into the window as the rebbe entered the hut. A sick old woman was lying in bed. "But I have no money to pay for the wood," the woman replied. "I still didn't pay you for the last batch you brought."

"Don't worry," the rebbe assured her as he put the wood next to the stove. "You don't have to pay me till you have the money. Meanwhile, take this wood. It will keep you warm this winter." He then lit the stove and prepared a bowl of soup for the old woman.

The Rebbe of Nemirov slipped out of the house and hurried home.

The next day, Yankel told the people how he had followed the rebbe home to see him rise up to heaven.

"Did he really rise up to heaven?" the people asked.

Yankel smiled and said, "Our rebbe didn't just rise up to heaven yesterday. He rose even higher!"

ROSH HASHANAH
The Scale

In the village of Pachkow it had not rained all year. The river was dry. The trees, the grass and the plants were dying. Everyone was thirsty and hungry.

"The entire town must fast and pray to Hashem for rain," the rabbi told the people. "Only Hashem can save us."

Still no rain came. Still the ground was dry.

"It must be me who is at fault," thought the rabbi. "I will fast and pray even harder, and maybe Hashem will help us."

That night the rabbi had a dream. In his dream Hashem said, "Rosh Hashanah is coming and Kalman the storekeeper must be the *chazzan* on the day before Rosh Hashanah."

The rabbi awoke. "Kalman the storekeeper? But Kalman can barely read! He can't lead the service. It must have been a false dream."

The next night, the rabbi had the same dream. Hashem again told him that Kalman the storekeeper must be the *chazzan* on the day before Rosh Hashanah.

That morning the rabbi awoke. "I had the same dream twice. It must be true."

In shul that morning, the rabbi approached Kalman and said, "You will be the *chazzan* on the day before Rosh Hashanah."

Kalman sat and stared at the rabbi. "You must be mistaken, rabbi. I can hardly read the words of the *davening*. I cannot lead the prayers."

"There is no choice," the rabbi replied. "You will lead the prayers."

Kalman took off his *tallis* and *tefillin* and rushed out of *shul*. Everyone waited in silence, not sure what would happen next.

A short while later, Kalman returned, holding the scale from his store in his hand. He walked up to the *aron kodesh* and said, "Hashem, this is the scale from my store. I promise that I have never charged even one person unfairly on it. On Rosh Hashanah our deeds are put on a scale. Please have pity on us when we are measured on Your scale."

A few moments later, a boom of thunder was heard outside. Everyone ran out and watched the rains finally start falling. Because of Kalman's purity and honesty, Hashem had mercy on the people and brought the rain.

YOM KIPPUR
Where Is the Rav?

It was *Erev* Yom Kippur, the holiest day of the year. All the people were already in *shul*. Everyone sat quietly, reviewing his deeds of the past year. Each person knew that in heaven their fate was now being decided.

A murmuring could be heard throughout the room. The people were worried. "Where is the rabbi?" they asked. *Kol Nidrei* would be starting in a few minutes, and their beloved rav was not yet in *shul*.

"How could this be?" some asked.

"G-d forbid, did anything happen to him?" questioned others.

The sky was getting dark. The *gabbai* silently slipped out of *shul* to look for the rabbi.

He searched all over town, but could not find him anywhere. Finally the *gabbai* heard a sweet humming melody coming from a house. As he peeked through the window, he saw the rav inside with a little girl and a baby.

"Rabbi, what are you doing here? It is time for *Kol Nidrei*," stammered the *gabbai*. "I've been looking all over for you. Everyone is in *shul* waiting for you."

"Shh," said the rav. "This little girl and I have been rocking the baby in the cradle for the last half hour. He just stopped crying and is about to fall asleep."

"But rebbe, the whole town is in *shul*, waiting for you."

"I was on my way to *shul* when I heard a baby cry," the rav explained. "I knocked on the door, and this little girl answered. Her parents had gone to *shul* and left her in charge of her baby brother. But he woke up and she couldn't calm him down, so I came in to help."

"But it's Yom Kippur. What about *Kol Nidrei*?" insisted the *gabbai*.

"How could I go to *shul* and leave this little baby crying?" the Rav asked.

Now that the baby was asleep, the Rav left with the *gabbai* to *daven Kol Nidrei* together with the rest of the town.

Siddur of Tears

oske grew up in a small village deep in the mountains of Russia. He was raised in a happy home, but his heart was not at peace. He often had strange dreams, dreams of another home in a different place with a different family.

"Why do I have these dreams?" Moske asked his father.

"Shhh, my son, just sleep now. They are nothing," he replied.

But the father watched the boy become more and more unhappy. He decided it was time to tell Moske the truth. "Moske, we are not your real parents. My wife and I rescued you from a band of Cossacks who killed your whole family. You are Jewish. That is why you have those dreams about another family." He then showed Moske a few things that he and his wife had taken from Moske's house.

One item caught Moske's attention — a small leather book.

"What is this?" Moske asked. "What is this strange writing here inside the book?"

"I don't know, Moske," the father replied. "Let's go ask the rabbi."

The father told the rabbi the whole story. The rabbi stroked his beard. "This writing inside the book, Moske, is your mother's name. This was her prayer book. Tonight is the holiday of Yom Kippur, the holiest day of the Jewish year. Would you join us in the synagogue tonight?"

The father sat there listening to the rabbi. Upon leaving the rabbi's house, he turned to Moske and said, "The time has come for you to learn about your people. Take your mother's book and go to the synagogue tonight."

That night, Moske entered the synagogue. He watched the people around him. He kissed his mother's book and clutched it close to his chest. Tears streamed down his cheeks. "Please G-d, I know little of my people and nothing of my true parents. All I have is this prayer book. Take these strange letters written here and turn them into the words I need to talk to You."

The rabbi saw Moske crying in the back of the *shul*. He came over to comfort him. "Tonight come join me and my family in my house across the yard and learn about the Jewish people. And bring your mother's prayer book with you."

SUCCOS

The Holy Succah

The Rebbe of Rachmastrivk, R' Mordechai Twerski, was a holy man. "The time has come for me to move to *Eretz Yisrael*," he decided one day. Since it was a very long journey from Ukraine, he brought very little with him. But there was one thing he would not leave behind — his father's succah.

This succah was very special. Many great Torah leaders had celebrated the holiday inside it. One could feel holiness in its very walls. Before Rabbi Twerski left Poland, a rich man offered to buy the succah from him. The rich man understood how special this succah was. "I will pay you any price, just sell me your holy succah," the man begged. But the rebbe would not sell it. "This succah is my treasure," he answered. "It was given to me by my father."

When he arrived in *Eretz Yisrael*, Reb Mordechai moved to Jerusalem. His first winter there was unusually cold. Next door to the rebbe lived a little girl named Chanah. That winter she became very sick. Her family was poor. They did not have enough money to buy firewood to heat their house. But Chanah needed to be warm to get better.

Every day the rebbe came to visit her. "How are you feeling today, Chanah?" he asked.

"May Hashem bring you a quick and full recovery." But every day little Chanah became sicker. The rebbe prayed and prayed for her, but nothing seemed to help.

"If only we had money to buy firewood," Chanah's worried parents told the rebbe. "Maybe then she would get better."

The rebbe ran back to his house and opened his storage cabinet. He saw his precious succah sitting there. "There is no choice," he thought. He grabbed an axe and chopped up the succah into many small pieces. The rebbe brought this wood to Chanah's house.

"Here, I have this extra firewood in my house," he told her parents. "Please use it to heat your home. With Hashem's help, Chanah will have a speedy recovery."

The parents gratefully accepted his gift, not knowing that it was the wood from his cherished succah. And that week, Chanah had a complete recovery from her illness.

SUCCOS
One Leads to the Next

hat is that thing?" asked Mr. Hartman.

"I never saw anything like it in my life," answered Mr. Freiman.

A dozen men from Cedar Park, North Carolina, were standing around Yonasan's succah. Fourteen-year-old Yonasan had just returned home from Yeshivah Eitz Chaim for Succos. It was his first year away in yeshivah. When he came home, he wanted to build a succah. His parents agreed. Yonasan and his father worked hard to finish building their first succah. There had never been a succah in Cedar Park; no one there had ever seen one before.

"What do you do with that?" "How long will it be there?" "What is it for?" the men asked.

Dozens of questions were being thrown at Yonasan from all sides. He had no chance to answer even one.

"Why don't you all come to our succah later this evening?" suggested Yonasan. "Tonight is the first night of Succos, and there will be plenty of time to answer all of your questions then."

That night, so many neighbors gathered at Yonasan's little succah that they had to move outside. They all crowded together, anxious to find out why Yonasan had built this strange little house.

Yonasan told them the story of Succos. He explained how the Jewish people were freed from slavery. While they were in the desert they built little huts for shade, and Hashem protected them with his Clouds of Glory. Hashem told them to build little huts to remember this. He also explained the laws of *lulav* and *esrog*. This was all new to everyone. No one had heard any of this before.

As the people were leaving that night, one of them said, "I learned a lot tonight. Maybe it is time for us to start learning something about being more Jewish."

"What about hiring a rabbi to come live here?" asked another.

"And then we could open a school so our children can learn," suggested a third.

Yonasan listened to the men and smiled. He had learned in yeshivah that when we do one mitzvah, it always leads to another. He was surprised, though, how quickly the building of his succah would lead to so many other mitzvos.

CHANUKAH
Blackout!

t was the first night of Chanukah. Ilana and Yossi had just moved into a new neighborhood close to their Grandma Bella. She lived alone, and the children wanted to be with her to light the first candle.

"Thank you both for coming to celebrate Chanukah with me," Grandma Bella said. "You are such wonderful grandchildren. But it is dark now and time for both of you to go home."

"We're so glad we moved into our new house and don't live far away from you anymore," Ilana said as she kissed her grandmother good-bye.

The two children began walking home. Suddenly there was a bright flash of lightning in the sky and then a loud crashing noise. All the streetlights went out.

"It's a blackout!" yelled Yossi. "And there isn't even a moon tonight, because it is so cloudy. I can hardly see anything."

"I'm scared," Ilana shivered. "And I'm very cold."

"Don't worry," Yossi reassured her. "We'll find our way home."

The two children continued walking, but in the dark, nothing looked familiar. The more they walked, the more lost they felt.

"I don't recognize any of these houses, do you?" Ilana asked.

"Don't worry, we'll find our way soon," Yossi comforted her. But he, too, was beginning to feel afraid.

"Look, there is a light," shouted Ilana. "Do you see it?"

"It can't be," Yossi replied. "We're having a power blackout. There are no lights."

"But look, it *is* a light," Ilana insisted.

Yossi stared into the distance. Sure enough, he did see a small flickering light very far away. "You're right," Yossi said. "It is a light. Let's walk in that direction."

As the children came closer to the light, they began to see more lights twinkling. "Those are all Chanukah candles," Yossi shouted in joy. "We are back in our own neighborhood."

Yossi and Ilana found their way home, following the lit Chanukah candles. That year they had their own little Chanukah miracle, a miracle of lights.

CHANUKAH
Lost and Found

"**S**hlomo Klein, clean up your room now," his mother shouted. "Please get rid of all your things lying around on the floor."

"Okay, Mom," he called back. "I'll do it right now."

Shlomo picked up everything on the floor and under his bed. He threw much of it into the garbage.

That afternoon, Meir, Shlomo's friend next door, saw a big pile of garbage sitting out on the street. "What is this?" Meir thought, as he picked up a dull piece of metal. "I'll take it home and clean it up."

Meir spent that whole week fixing, rubbing, and polishing his great find. It soon began to shine and looked as good as new.

"Shlomo, don't forget that tonight is Chanukah," Mrs. Klein said. "Please be sure to get your menorah ready so we can all light candles together."

"Oh no," Shlomo answered. "I don't have it anymore. I threw it out last week when I cleaned my room. It was so old and rusty."

"That is really a shame," his mother said. "I'm afraid this year you won't be able to light your own Chanukah candles."

Feeling sad, Shlomo went next door to visit his friend Meir. "Meir, what is that you are holding in your hand?" Shlomo asked.

"You won't believe it," Meir replied. "Someone threw out this great menorah. I always wanted one, but my parents couldn't afford to buy it for me. It didn't look so good when I found it last week. It was old and rusty. But I spent the last few days shining it, and now it looks as good as new."

Shlomo stared at the menorah. He couldn't believe what he was seeing. "That's my menorah. Give it back to me. When I threw it out, it was old and rusty, but now it looks beautiful. I want it back."

"But I found it and it's mine," said Meir. "You threw it out."

Shlomo thought for a minute. "You are right," he said. "You should keep the menorah. You found it, and it really is yours."

That night, when it was time to light Chanukah candles, Shlomo joined his family. He turned to his mother and smiled, "For the first time, my friend Meir finally has his own menorah. He always wanted one. I am so happy for him."

ROSH CHODESH
Capture the Moon

In the village of Chelm, the people were very silly. But they also were very poor.

Lempel, the mayor of Chelm, had an idea how to make money. "Every month," he explained, "Jews all over the world bless the new moon. If we could capture the moon, we would be able to rent it out to everyone in nearby villages. We would never be poor again."

"Brilliant idea!" squealed his assistant, Shlempel. "Let's do it. But how will you capture the moon?" he asked in wonder.

Lempel knew just what he needed to do. "Get me a large barrel and fill it to the top with borscht," he ordered. Shlempel did as he was told. "Now look inside the barrel," Lempel insisted. Shlempel looked inside the barrel and saw a reflection of the moon in there, shining bright.

"You did it!" shouted Shlempel. "You captured the moon in the barrel."

"Now quickly seal the barrel. When the time comes to bless the new moon, we will open the barrel and rent out the moon."

"Brilliant idea," shouted Shlempel in joy. "There is no mayor like the mayor of Chelm."

That month the whole town of Chelm worked very hard on their new business venture. They printed up business cards, brochures, and catalogs, and sent them to all the other villages. Signs stating *Rent-a-moon from the village of Chelm* were hung on walls all over the countryside.

Finally, the new month came. That morning, everyone crowded around the barrel, waiting to see the moon caught inside. Lempel the mayor undid the seal and opened it. Everyone looked in, but saw nothing except some sticky old borscht.

"Oh, no. Where is the moon?" everyone shouted. "How could this have happened? Did someone steal it?"

Lempel stroked his forehead, deep in thought. "The moon must have dissolved in the borscht," he explained. "I'm afraid we will have to pour the borscht out into the street. This month, we won't be able to rent out the moon."

And that night, there was no joy in the village of Chelm. All their plans of riches were poured right down the drain.

TU BISHEVAT
Dani's Tree

Dani loved looking out his window to watch his favorite tree. In the summer he sat under it, enjoying the shade.

One day Dani decided to build a model airplane out of wood. "But where will I get the wood?" he wondered. "I know. I'll cut a branch off my tree and use the wood. There are so many more branches, it won't matter if one is missing."

Dani cut off a branch and used it to build a model airplane.

The tree still gave him shade in the summer.

When Dani got a bit older, he decided to build a birdhouse. "But where will I get the wood?" he wondered. "I'll cut a few branches off my tree and use that wood. There are so many more branches, it won't matter if a few are missing."

Dani cut off a few branches and used them to build a birdhouse.

When Dani grew older, he decided to build a porch for his house. "But where will I get the wood?" he wondered. "I'll use the wood from my favorite tree."

Dani cut down the tree and used the wood to build the porch.

When Dani looked out his window the next morning, he realized his tree was gone. All that was left was a stump. "How could I have cut down my favorite tree?" he thought. "Now it is gone forever." He felt very sad.

A year passed. Dani looked out his window and thought, "Today is Tu BiShevat, the New Year for trees. I'm sorry I cut down my tree. I miss sitting under it."

He walked outside and sat on the stump. Suddenly he saw a small green bud growing out of the bark. "A new bud," he happily shouted. "It's a new bud. My tree is still alive. One day it will grow again. I am so happy."

It would take many years for his tree to grow, but he knew that even if *he* couldn't enjoy it anymore, one day his children would.

PURIM
Who Is Right?

ankel and Yentel were married for ten years, but still argued every day. If Yankel said, "What a nice day it is," Yentel replied, "To me, it looks like it will rain." When Yentel said, "See how nice and clean the house is," Yankel would answer, "But look at that dirty window."

It was the day before Purim. "The time has come to prepare *shalach manos*," Yankel told his wife. "This year, let us give a delicious *hamantasch* with a bottle of wine to our friends."

"Oh no," said Yentel. "It would be much better to give them challah and a bottle of grape juice." All night the two argued back and forth, each showing why his or her idea was better.

Morning came, and Yankel returned home from *shul*. Both of them still could not agree what to give for *shalach manos*. "I have an idea," Yankel finally said. "Let us go to our wise rabbi. He will show you how right I am."

"That's a good idea," Yentel replied. "Now you will find out how smart your wife really is."

The couple came to the rav's house. "Don't you see?" Yankel explained to the rav. "It is clearly preferable to give a *hamantasch* and wine for *shalach manos*."

The wise rabbi listened and stroked his beard. "Yankel, you are right. There is no question about it. But what about Yentel?"

Yentel then explained why it would be better, instead, to give challah with a bottle of grape juice.

The rabbi closed his eyes deep in thought. "Yentel, everything you say is true. I see that *you* are right."

The rebbetzin was sitting in the kitchen, listening to the whole conversation. Unable to control her curiosity any longer, she entered the room and said to her husband, "First you said Yankel was right. Then you said Yentel was right. Both of them cannot be right!"

The rabbi rubbed his forehead, swaying from side to side. "You know, my dear wife, I see that you are right, too."

Meanwhile, a happy Yankel and Yentel had left the rabbi's house. Both were smiling, knowing that they were right. That year, for *shalach manos* they gave a bottle of grape juice, a bottle of wine, a challah and a *hamantasch*.

PURIM
The Costume

hirah, what will you be wearing this Purim?" Beth asked.

"Shirah, wait till you see my new Queen Esther costume," Zohar added.

"Shirah, I'm going dressed up as an elf," chimed in Mindy.

All day Shirah heard about the exciting costumes everyone else would be wearing this Purim. But she was sad. She didn't have a costume for Purim. Her family hardly had enough money to buy food, let alone buy Purim costumes.

"Mommy," cried Shirah, "everyone in my class has such wonderful costumes for Purim. And I don't have anything. Why can't I have a costume like everyone else? I wish Purim would never come this year." Her eyes moistened with tears.

"There must be something I can give my daughter," Mrs. Berman thought. "We don't have enough money to buy new costumes. But there must be something I can do for her."

Shirah slowly walked to her room to do her homework. Her cheeks were still damp with tears.

Mrs. Berman ran up to the attic. She dragged out a big chest covered with dust. Opening it, she found just what she was looking for. She lifted it out of the chest and took it downstairs to the den.

Mrs. Berman spent the next six hours sitting over her sewing machine, altering, pinning and sewing. This had to be done just right. This had to come out perfect.

The next morning, Mrs. Berman went upstairs to wake up Shirah for school. In her arms, she carried her own wedding dress. She had spent all night getting it ready. "Here is your Purim costume for

this year. I really hope you like it."

Shirah stared at the beautiful wedding dress. Her eyes opened
wide and a large smile spread across her face. "Mommy, this is the
best costume I have ever seen. Thank you so much." Shirah couldn't
wait for Purim to arrive.

PESACH

A Knock at the Door

The Frankels were having their first *Seder*. They lived in Russia when the Communists did not let Jews be religious. Until this year they barely knew they were Jewish. But eight months ago, Mordechai, the father, began secretly studying with a rabbi. "This is our first *Seder* in Russia," Mordechai told his wife and three children, "and I hope it will be our last one here. Next year may we have our *Seder* in Jerusalem."

The table was set with a *Seder* plate, wine and matzos. The family shared one Haggadah. Mother had secretly baked the matzos.

Mordechai began telling the story of the Jews leaving Egypt. "Thirty-three hundred years ago, the Jewish people were slaves in Egypt. They worked very hard and never had a chance to rest. But they prayed and had faith in Hashem, and one day He took them out of slavery and led them into the land of Israel."

The three children listened carefully to every word. They had never heard these stories before. It was all very new and exciting to them.

"And if we have faith and pray to G-d," the father continued, "then Hashem will rescue us, too, and bring us out of Russia to Israel, just as he did thousands of years ago."

Suddenly there was a loud knock at the door. The room became very quiet. It was against the law to have a *Seder* in Russia. Everyone was afraid it was the police. Then the family would be arrested and put in jail.

The pounding on the door continued. "What should we do, Father?" Michael, the youngest son, whispered.

"Just have faith in Hashem," the father calmly replied. "We saw in the Haggadah how He saved the Jews then. He can save us now, also."

The banging on the door did not stop. "Go and answer the door, Michael," the father said. "Each of us should pray to Hashem."

Michael got up from the table and walked to the door. "Please help us, Hashem," trembled Michael. Slowly he opened the door.

"Who is there?" called the father.

But Michael just stood there staring. The hall was empty. Then they heard the siren of a police car traveling away into the distance. No one knew why the police had left. That year, the Frankel family celebrated their own Pesach miracle.

PESACH
Turkish Silk

t was *Erev* Pesach in Berditchev. Reb Levi Yitzchak called his *shamash* into his study. "Berel, I want you to do me a favor. Please go and bring me some Turkish silk."

"Turkish silk?" Berel stared at the rebbe in amazement. "You know I would do anything you ask, but it is against the law to buy Turkish silk. Our country is at war with Turkey, and it is illegal to own anything from there."

"I am well aware of that," said Reb Levi Yitzchak, "but please go out and get me some Turkish silk."

Berel left the rebbe's study and returned in just fifteen minutes, holding a leather pouch. "Here, Rebbe, I brought you some Turkish silk."

"Thank you," said the rebbe. "But Berel, how did you get it so quickly?"

"It was really quite simple," the *shamash* replied. "Even though it is illegal, you can buy Turkish silk in any alleyway or basement."

"Now I have one more favor to ask you," said Reb Levi Yitzchak. "Please go to any of the Jewish homes and bring me back a slice of bread."

"A slice of bread just before Pesach?" Berel couldn't believe what he was hearing. But the rebbe asked, so Berel did as he was told.

A few hours later Berel returned empty-handed. "Rebbe, I went to all the Jewish homes asking for bread. They don't even have crumbs!"

The rebbe smiled and looked up to heaven. "Do you see, Hashem, what the Jewish people are like? The czar made laws that no Turkish silk may be bought in Russia. There are policemen to enforce these laws. And yet you can walk into any home and buy Turkish silk.

"Three thousand years ago you told the Jewish people they could

not have any chametz in their house during Pesach. No bread for an entire week. No police enforce Your laws, yet not one crumb of chametz can be found in this entire town. Do you see how wonderful Your Jewish people are?"

LAG B'OMER
The Big Game

he day had finally arrived. Naftali woke up and saw the sun shining brightly. It was Lag B'Omer, the day of the school picnic. But more important, it was the day of the big baseball game. His sixth grade class was playing against the sixth grade class of another yeshivah. This was the game the whole school, and many parents, would come to watch.

Everyone boarded the bus for the half-hour ride to Comston Park. Outside the city, the leaves on the trees were already green and the flowers bloomed. "I'll be playing center field," thought Naftali. "I'll be the star of the game."

But at that same moment, his classmate, Yoni, was having his own dreams. "Lag B'Omer is finally here," thought Yoni. "Today is the big game, and I'm going to be playing in center field."

Everyone got off the bus. The teachers began preparing food for the picnic. The sixth grade boys ran straight to the baseball field to begin practice. Both Naftali and Yoni stood together in center field.

"Yoni, don't you know, I'm playing center field today," said Naftali.

"Oh no," insisted Yoni. "I've been dreaming about this game all year. I'm going to play center field."

"But I'm the better hitter," Naftali persisted.

"But I'm the better fielder," Yoni countered. The two boys began arguing.

The team captain came over. "What are you two fighting about? The game starts in fifteen minutes. Work it out!"

Naftali turned to Yoni. "Do you know what day today is?"

"It's Lag B'Omer," Yoni replied. "The day of our big game."

"But do you remember what Lag B'Omer means?" Naftali asked. "Almost 2,000 years ago, 24,000 students of Rabbi Akiva died in a plague. They died because they didn't respect one another and fought with each other. On Lag B'Omer the plague ended. That is why today is a day of happiness and fun."

The two boys looked at each other. "You're right," said Yoni. "We should not be arguing with each other."

"I have an idea," Naftali suggested. "Why don't we switch off. You play center field for the first half of the game, and I'll play center field for the second half." The boys smiled at each other and began practice.

SHAVUOS
The Dream

Betzalel wanted to stay up the whole night. Tonight was Shavuos and he knew that people stayed up all night to learn Torah. But he was only ten years old, and had never stayed up that late before.

"But I really want to stay up the whole night to learn," Betzalel explained to his parents.

"That is very nice," his mother answered, "but aren't you a little young for that?"

"I have an idea," said his father. "Why don't you go take a nap now. Then come with me to *shul* tonight and you can stay up until you are tired and ready to fall asleep." This idea pleased Betzalel very much.

That night Betzalel walked to *shul* with his father. The two sat down and began learning together. Both father and son were very happy.

But at 11:00 Betzalel started yawning. His eyes became heavy. He yawned again, and it became harder and harder for him to think.

"I'll just shut my eyes for a few seconds," Betzalel thought. "Then, in a few minutes, I'll be ready to learn again."

He closed his eyes and fell fast asleep. He dreamed that he saw Moshe Rabbeinu sitting at the head of a long table. Seated around him were all the great leaders of the generations. Rabbi Akiva, Hillel, Rambam and many others were all gathered around, learning together.

"Why don't you come join us?" Moshe called to Betzalel.

Betzalel was in awe. "These great men want me to sit and learn with them?" he wondered.

"Tonight is Shavuos," Moshe explained. "Thousands of years ago, on this day, our holy Torah was given. We saw how much you wanted to learn tonight. It would be our pleasure if you sat here and learned together with us."

Betzalel took a seat between Rashi and the Vilna Gaon. He sat and listened to Moshe teach the Torah.

Suddenly, Betzalel heard a loud bang on the table. "It is time to *daven Shacharis*," a man called out. He awoke with a start from his dream. But what a dream it was. "I may have fallen asleep," Betzalel told his father, "but you wouldn't believe how much I learned tonight."

SHAVUOS
The Angels' Complaint

Moshe Rabbeinu went up to heaven to receive the Torah from Hashem. For forty days and forty nights Hashem taught him the Torah.

When the angels discovered that Moshe was receiving the Torah, they complained to Hashem, "How can You give Your holy Torah to a human? Thousands of years before You created the world, Your Torah was here in heaven. Why do You now give it to the Jewish people? Let it stay here with us."

Hashem turned to Moshe and commanded him, "Answer them!"

Moshe became frightened. "How can I answer them? I am afraid they will burn me up if I open my mouth."

"Take hold of My holy throne and answer them," Hashem reassured him.

Moshe turned to the angels and spoke. "Let us see what is inside the Torah that Hashem is giving the Jewish people. It says, 'I took you out of Egypt.' Were you angels ever in Egypt? Did you suffer there as slaves?"

The angels replied that they did not.

Then Moshe continued, "The Torah says, 'You shall not worship any other gods.' Do you, angels, worship any god other than Hashem?"

And the angels agreed that they did not.

Moshe continued. "The Torah says, 'Remember the Sabbath to keep it holy.' Do angels do any work from which they need to rest?"

The angels agreed that they did not.

"The Torah commands, 'Honor your father and your mother.' Do angels have a father or a mother to honor?"

The angels admitted that they did not.

Then Moshe ended by saying, "Angels cannot murder, they cannot steal, there is no jealousy among them. This is what is written in the

Torah. This proves that the Torah is not for you, it is meant for man."

The angels now understood that the Torah was, indeed, for man, and all the angels became friends with Moshe. Moshe then went down to earth and brought the Torah to the Jewish people.

ROSH CHODESH
The Sun and the Moon

On the fourth day of creation, Hashem made the sun and the moon. Both were the same size and were equally bright. Both shone down upon the earth and warmed it with their rays. This was fine with the sun, but the moon was not happy.

"Why should the sun and I both be the same size?" the moon complained to Hashem. "It would be better if you made the sun smaller and less bright than I. Then I would be the ruler of the skies."

Hashem was disappointed. It was just the beginning of creation, and already there was fighting and jealousy.

"I will teach you a lesson," said Hashem. "You don't want to be the same size as the sun; then so be it. Make yourself smaller!"

And the moon became much smaller in size.

The moon became very upset. "Hashem," it cried, "look at me. I am so small and powerless now. Please forgive me. It was wrong of me to complain. I was wrong to want to be bigger and more powerful than the sun."

Hashem listened to the moon's pleas for forgiveness. He felt sorry for the moon. "Moon, you have humbled yourself. Each month," Hashem promised, "the Jewish people will look up to the heavens and watch for you to know when to celebrate their holidays. Their calendar will be based upon you. Each *Rosh Chodesh* the Jewish people will bring a special offering in the *Beis HaMikdash*."

"In addition to this," Hashem decreed, "the moon will be the ruler of the skies at night. Every night when the moon appears, all the stars will also appear with it. And every morning when the moon disappears, all the stars will disappear with it."

Once again there was peace in the skies.

TISHAH B'AV
Truth over Everything

t was Tishah B'Av morning, a day of fasting. Reb Levi Yitzchak of Berditchev sat deep in thought. "What a sad day it is. The *Beis HaMikdash* was destroyed almost 1,700 years ago. To me, it feels like it happened only yesterday."

Walking to *shul*, he saw a Jew walking down the street and eating.

"My friend," Rabbi Levi Yitzchak said, "I see you are eating. You must have forgotten that today is Tishah B'Av, a very serious fast day. It was on this day that our Holy Temple was destroyed. We are not allowed to eat any food all day."

"Oh, of course I know that it is Tishah B'Av," the man answered. "Every Jew knows that!"

"Then you must be ill," Reb Levi Yitzchak continued, "and that is why you are eating today. Your doctor must have told you not to fast."

"No, Rabbi," the man replied. "I feel fine. To tell you the truth, I never felt better in my whole life."

"Then no doubt you were brought up in a place where you were not taught the holiness and sorrow of the day. Please come to *shul* with me and learn what happened to the Jewish people on Tishah B'Av," insisted Reb Levi Yitzchak.

"Oh no, Rabbi," the man persisted. "I know all about the laws of Tishah B'Av."

Reb Levi Yitzchak stared at the man. Then he looked up to heaven. "King of the Universe," he said, "look how holy your Jewish people are. This man could have lied to me, and given any excuse he wanted. But rather than tell a lie, he told the truth. How could you not forgive the Jews for their sins? There is no one like the Jewish people!"

The man was so impressed with Reb Levi Yitzchak that he stopped eating and followed him into *shul*.

Glossary

aron kodesh	the ark in the synagogue, where the Torah Scrolls are kept
Beis HaMikdash	the Holy Temple in Jerusalem
chametz	leaven, which one may not eat, own or benefit from on Passover
chazzan	leader of the prayers
daven(ing)	pray(ing)
Eretz Yisrael	Land of Israel
erev	the day before
esrog	a citron; used on Succos
gabbai	person responsible for the running of a synagogue; a rabbi's assistant
hamantasch	a special, three-cornered, filled cake made for Purim
Kol Nidrei	prayer at the beginning of Yom Kippur
kugel	pudding
lulav	a palm branch; used on Succos
Rosh Chodesh	beginning of a month in the Hebrew calendar
shalach manos	portions of food given as gifts on Purim
Seder	The festive meal eaten on the first two nights of Passover (in Israel only the first night)
Selichos	prayers said on the days around the time of Rosh Hashanah
Shacharis	morning prayers
shamash	person who maintains care of the synagogue; a caretaker
shul	synagogue
tallis	prayer shawl
tefillin	leather boxes containing Torah portions, worn by men during weekday morning prayers
zemiros	Shabbos songs